WIZARDS, WARRIORS & YOU
is a game of fantasy role-playing
as w

In each adven   the
game as either t   ring
the Wizard's rou   ical
spells to fend off your enemies. Carrying the Warrior's sword, you will use your strength and bril-
liance in battle to prevail against all challengers.

There are dozens of adventures in this book. If
you choose to play the role of the Wizard, all of
the mysterious spells in *The Book of Spells* at the
back of this book will be at your command. Use
them to guide the Wizard past peril after peril.

Then close the book and start all over again,
this time as the Warrior. Try your skill with all
of the weapons listed in *The Book of Weapons*, also
found at the back of this book.

**No matter which role you choose to play, you
will face new challenges, battle surprising foes,
and make life-or-death decisions on every page!**

Avon Books in the
WIZARDS, WARRIORS & YOU™ SERIES

WIZARDS, WARRIORS & YOU™

BOOK 5

The Haunted Castle of Ravencurse

by Lynn Beach
illustrated by Earl Norem
A Parachute Press Book

AVON
PUBLISHERS OF BARD, CAMELOT, DISCUS AND FLARE BOOKS

**To Matthew, Christine, Alexander,
Ole, Mark, and Andrew Kjolsrud**

WIZARDS, WARRIORS & YOU™: THE HAUNTED CAS-
TLE OF RAVENCURSE is an original publication of Avon
Books. This work has never before appeared in book form.

AVON BOOKS
A division of
The Hearst Corporation
1790 Broadway
New York, New York 10019

Introduction

Past the pale stone castle, where King Henry rules, past the green courtyard where Henry's knights train and meet in the competition of the joust, past the meadows where the King's cows graze, past the vineyards where the King's wine is pressed, past the marketplace, past the village inns, past the farms, several hundred yards beyond the low brick wall that forms the very boundary of the royal domain, stands a large, flat rock.

This rock is bounded by a steep, jagged cliff on one side and the rolling purple ocean on the other. It is on this flat rock that the Wizard and the Warrior meet to remember adventures of the past and to talk of adventures yet to come.

They have much to talk about.

Together, this team of legend — this master of magical forces and this champion of the lightning sword — have defeated evil in this world and in worlds beyond. They have triumphed over untold foes in castles and courtyards, and in the mountains and forests that surround the medieval world.

The challenges of this world are many. For there are always those — human and nonhuman — who would destroy the Wizard and the Warrior and the world they protect.

You are about to enter this world of danger and adventure. As the Wizard or the Warrior, you will decide how to face each challenge.

If you make the right decisions, the Wizard and the Warrior will succeed in their quest, and their legend will live on. If you make the wrong choices, their bright legend will dim — and you will find yourself trapped in a world of unimagined horrors.

The journey into the world of *Wizards, Warriors, and You* begins on page 1.

1

On the top of a jagged cliff stands an ancient, mist-shrouded castle. Its crumbling stone walls are covered with dripping green moss, and the only sound to be heard from within is the sinister call of a raven.

Hundreds of years ago, a trail wound up the cliff, but that trail has vanished. Now the only way to reach the castle is to climb the sheer face of the cliff. Its surface is like glass. Legends claim it is guarded by trolls and the deadly Cyclops of the Cliff. Surely, those unlucky enough — or foolish enough — to risk entering the castle take their lives in their hands.

At the foot of the cliff stand the dauntless Wizard and Warrior. As they look up at the castle, wondering what lies in wait for them, they remember the fateful day that sent them here.

Both the Wizard and the Warrior were well-rested from their last mission as they joined King Henry in his throne room. However, they could not help but notice that the monarch himself looked careworn and tired.

"My good friends," King Henry said, "I must burden you with a grave problem. As you know, our kingdom has fought many wars in recent years. These struggles have worn out my people and cost us dearly. The royal treasury is nearly depleted, but I cannot raise taxes again without causing great suffering to the poor. And yet, we must maintain our defenses and be ever ready to fight new enemies."

"You may count on my sword always," said the Warrior.

"My magic is ever at your service," said the Wizard.

"I know, my friends, and I am grateful. And that is why I am going to ask you to undertake another quest. Before you agree, I must warn you that this may be the most dangerous mission you have ever faced. The perils are many and unknown, and they are from the spirit world as well as the real. But the reward is great, too. The reward is treasure enough to fill the royal coffers ten times over."

The King reached beneath his throne and removed a black box. Attached to its obsidian surface was the carved image of a raven. "This is the Crested Casket of Ravencurse," he told the heroes. "It came into my family a hundred years ago. It was brought to us by a servant of the ancient Ravencurse family."

King Henry sighed, then continued, "This family, who lived in a castle near the mountain town of Ravencurse, was known for generations for their fabulous wealth — and for their awesome evil. All of them were monstrously cruel. The most evil Ravencurse of all was the last, Mad Morwenna. She was a powerful sorceress, said to be the most beautiful woman in the land, with hair as dark as a raven's wing. But she went mad one night and created unearthly monsters who slaughtered all of her family and servants. One only escaped, and came to us, bringing this box."

"What happened to Mad Morwenna?" asked the Wizard.

"Nobody knows," said the King. "Legend has it that she was never seen again after that horrible night. No one has entered the castle in the one hundred years since Mad Morwenna's terrible deed. It is said that she put a curse on the castle to prevent anyone from stealing the treasures of Ravencurse. The evil guardians she called from the dark live there still. It is said that her ghost walks the halls of the castle."

Then the King handed the obsidian box to the Warrior. "In this chest is a map drawn by the servant who was the sole survivor. It shows the part of the castle that holds the Ravencurse treasures and gives some indication of the monsters that may be guarding them. Remember, this map is very old, and the servant was still shaken with terror when she drew it. It may not be complete."

The Warrior pulled out the map and showed it to the Wizard. Their brows knitted in concentration as they studied the faded document.

"I cannot order you to undertake this perilous mission," King Henry continued. "I would not even ask, were it not for the state of the treasury."

"Fear not," said the Warrior. "Together we will go to the Castle of Ravencurse. Between my weapons and my friend's powerful magic, we will defeat Mad Morwenna and return with the treasures."

"You may count on it, Your Excellency," agreed the Wizard.

So this is how the brave friends find themselves here, at the base of the cliff below the Haunted Castle of Ravencurse. The story is now *your* story. It is up to *you* to battle the evil waiting in the castle and bring out the treasures. The time has come for you to choose the role you will play.

Will you take the part of the Wizard or the Warrior? Make your choice now, as you enter this world of *Wizards, Warriors, and You.*

If you choose to be the Wizard, turn to PAGE 10.
If you choose to be the Warrior, turn to PAGE 9.

CRIMSON CROWN →

DOOR

CELLAR

KITCHEN

BALLROOM

BOTTOMLE BASKET →

← ENTRANCE HALL

DOOR

○ ← STATUES

CLIFF

GROUND FLOOR PLAN of

HAUNTED CASTLE of RAVENCURSE

TREASURES OF RAVENCURSE

THE CRIMSON CROWN OF RAVENCURSE. CREATED FOR RUDOLF OF RAVENCURSE 500 YEARS AGO. MADE OF GOLD, SET WITH PRECIOUS RUBIES AND GARNETS, THE CROWN IS ENCHANTED: WHOEVER OWNS IT GAINS POWER TO MAKE CHOICES ABOUT MONEY AND TREASURE.

THE BOTTOMLESS BASKET OF RAVENCURSE. THIS BASKET WAS ORIGINALLY BROUGHT FROM THE LOST CONTINENT OF ATLANTIS. IT PROVIDES UNLIMITED WEALTH FOR ANYONE WHO IS NOT TOO GREEDY.

BEWARE THE EVIL GUARDIANS OF RAVENCURSE

GUARDING THE CASTLE: A TROLL, A CYCLOPS AND THE BLACK KNIGHT.
GUARDING THE CROWN: ZOMBIES.

GUARDING THE BASKET: SPIDER OF DOOM.

OTHER EVILS MAY APPEAR, IN OR OUT OF THE CASTLE. THEY INCLUDE: ENCHANTED RAVENS, GRIFFINS, A TWO-HEADED WOLF, DEADLY SPELLS AND ENCHANTMENTS, AND THE GHOST OF MAD MORWENNA.

The day is growing hot as you and the Wizard continue your climb. The cliff is not as steep here, and soon the top appears above you. Suddenly, you hear an eerie sound, as if a million wings were beating at once.

"Protect yourself!" cries the Wizard.

Looking up, you see hundreds of ravens descending. There are so many of them they blot out the sun. A chill runs through you as you realize they're flying in formation. Like a great dark curtain, they lift away from the side of the cliff and hover. Clearly, they're about to attack.

You look at your friend beneath you. The Wizard is holding onto the face of the cliff with both his hands and feet. He's in no position to cast a spell. You take inventory of your weapons. None of them seems suitable for fighting off hundreds of birds, yet you must try. Which one will work best?

Carefully, you reach behind you and draw one of the weapons you've chosen. Then you prepare to defend yourself and your companion against the ravens' talons.

If you chose the flail, the morning star, or the mace, turn to PAGE 21.

If you chose the battle-axe, lance, or crossbow, turn to PAGE 27.

If you chose any other weapon, turn to PAGE 18.

Instructions for the Warrior:

As you and your companion prepare to meet the fearsome dangers in the Haunted Castle of Raven-curse, you know that you will need to draw on all the strength and courage you possess. Although you do not know the precise nature of your foes, you have learned that the right weapon at the right time is a powerful ally.

At the back of this book, on page 101, you will find a book describing all the weapons you possess. In addition to the Sword of the Golden Lion, which is ever at your side, you may take *only three* of these weapons along with you on your mission. Study the map of the castle and the list of possible foes on pages 6 and 7. Then turn to *The Book of Weapons*. Choose carefully which three weapons you will take.

Turn to PAGE 15 to begin your perilous quest.

10

Instructions for the Wizard:

There is no telling what sort of magic you may meet in the Haunted Castle of Ravencurse. All you know is that you will be up against a foe whose sorcery may be as powerful as yours, and whose evil and cunning may exceed anything you have met in your many quests for King Henry.

At the back of this book, on page 97, you will find a book of all the magic spells you know how to summon up. Turn now to *The Book of Spells*. Read them over quickly so you will have an idea of the powers you can call on. Then study the map and list of foes on pages 6 and 7.

Now turn to PAGE 14 to begin your dangerous journey.

Walking quickly, you and the Warrior start up the trail, the bones crunching beneath your feet. "I wonder why there was no sign of this trail on the map," says your companion.

"Maybe it wasn't here when the map was drawn," you reply. You do not say so, but you wonder who could have cut this gruesome trail into the face of the cliff.

In a short time you are halfway up. Short, scrubby trees begin to appear around you. You estimate that at this rate it will take only a few more minutes to reach the Haunted Castle of Ravencurse.

Suddenly, your way is blocked by a manlike shape the size of an elephant. It is holding a staff made from the trunk of a large tree. In the center of its forehead gleams one large yellow eye.

"Halt!" calls the creature. "I am the Cyclops of the Cliff. No mortals may pass beyond this point!"

"That's what you think," says the Warrior, and he draws the Sword of the Golden Lion.

Quickly, you put your hand on his arm. You can see that the Cyclops greatly outmatches him. But it is too late. With an inhuman, booming laugh, the Cyclops raises its staff and strikes at the Warrior. Only his agility keeps your friend from being smashed as flat as a squashed ant.

Go on to PAGE 12.

The Warrior picks himself up and again approaches the Cyclops. Again he is knocked to the ground. After a moment, the Warrior pulls himself to his feet again. His arm trembling, he lifts his sword and prepares to attack.

"Stop!" you cry. "You have no chance!"

Now the Cyclops' booming laugh is directed at you. "Your friend has fallen under an enchantment," he says. "He is compelled to keep fighting until he — or his opponent — is dead. As you can see from the bones paving my trail, there is no question of the outcome. After I have finished with your friend, you will fight the same battle!"

To your horror, you see that the Cyclops has again lifted his staff and is aiming it at the Warrior. Your friend is bleeding and dazed, but he continues to fight. You know that he will soon die unless you do something to help him.

Quickly you review the spells you might use. You decide that the two most useful in this situation are Shrink and Invisibility. Which one do you use? Which is most likely to get the Warrior out of trouble?

If you decide to use the Shrink spell, turn to PAGE 22.

If you think Invisibility is more likely to work, go to PAGE 17.

You try to call to the Warrior to tell him not to shoot, but your voice isn't strong enough. You now have only one chance. Struggling weakly, you pull your cloak tighter around you, then you begin to whisper the Invisible Shield spell, to protect both the spider and yourself. You have no idea whether you are strong enough for the spell to work, but you must try.

To discover the outcome of the spell, count the number of letters in the name of the day on which you are reading this book. For example, Monday has six letters.

If the number is even, turn to **PAGE 45**.

If the number is odd, go to **PAGE 95**.

It is a brisk morning as you and the Warrior stand at the base of the cliff that leads to the Castle of Ravencurse. The cliff seems impossibly steep, rising almost straight up. You can barely see the top. It's clear that this will not be an easy climb. And you know that both you and your friend will need all your strength to battle the evils awaiting you in the castle.

"Perhaps there is an easier way up this cliff," you say to the Warrior. "Let us walk around it a bit."

Your friend agrees, and together you begin to walk to the south. Unfortunately, the cliff wall seems to be as sheer in this direction as in the other. You are about to give up when the Warrior points.

"Look!" he says. "There is a trail — leading upward."

You look, and hidden in some brush there is indeed a trail, which disappears into thick trees halfway up. As you approach, you notice that it is strewn with hundreds of oddly shaped white rocks. You pick one up, then drop it in horror. It is not a rock at all, but a bone from someone's finger! A broken skull lies at your feet. This trail is paved with thousands of human bones!

Should you take the trail? Or is it safer to try to climb up the cliff? Decide quickly.

If you decide to climb the cliff, turn to PAGE 71.

If you prefer to save your energy and take the trail — not knowing what you may meet — go to PAGE 11.

Along with your clever friend, the Wizard, you prepare to scale the jagged cliff that leads to the Castle of Ravencurse. Although at first glance the face of the cliff seems unclimbable, you soon see finger- and toeholds etched into the rock.

"This will not be an easy climb," says the Wizard, sounding worried.

"Follow me," you tell him. "I grew up in mountainous country like this."

You tie one end of a rope around your waist and another around the Wizard's waist. Then, after strapping your weapons to your back, you begin the perilous climb.

At first it is easier than you had expected. Soon the ground is far below you. Although the climb is proceeding smoothly, you keep your eyes and ears open for the troll that is said to guard the approach to the castle.

At last you reach a wide ledge. You help the Wizard onto it. You rest a moment, then you both notice that there is a dark cave leading into the cliff.

Go on to PAGE 16.

You turn to the Wizard and ask, "Do you think this could be an entrance to the castle? There is no sign of it on the map."

"The King warned us that the map may be incomplete," says the Wizard. "And if this does lead to the castle, it may be quicker than climbing."

"Yes," you agree, "but caves are often homes for trolls."

What do you do? Do you and the Wizard decide to enter the cave, hoping it is a shortcut to the castle? Or do you continue the long, dangerous climb?

If you decide to enter the cave, turn to PAGE 19.

If you choose to continue the climb, turn to PAGE 8.

No sooner have you finished casting the spell than there is a tremendous clap of thunder. When the aftershock has passed, you and your friend are both invisible.

At first the Cyclops looks confused, and then he begins to laugh even louder.

"Well done, Wizard!" he says. "Unfortunately, your spell of Invisibility will do you no good. Your friend cannot leave here until he has defeated me or been defeated. I have only to wait for the spell to wear off — and then I have you both!"

Too late, you realize that what the Cyclops has said is true. You are trying to decide on another spell when the Invisibility suddenly wears off.

The Cyclops swings his staff with all his might, and you shut your eyes. Better keep them shut — you do not want to see what he does to the Warrior and to you.

Alas, Wizard, this adventure has come to an early end. But you can always return by opening the book and again seeking the treasures of the Haunted Castle of Ravencurse.

END

18

Holding your weapon with one hand, you prepare to defend yourself from the vicious birds. Their shrieks grow louder, as if they anticipate sinking their talons into your flesh.

"Be ready for a change!" calls the Wizard below you. You look down. Somehow he has managed to wrap his cloak over himself, and he's reciting a spell to change you into a . . .

You feel a moment of dizziness, then suddenly you find yourself suspended in the air. Your black wings quickly take the wind as you spiral upward toward the top of the cliff. Your companion, also turned into a raven, soars beside you.

"We are safe now," the Wizard says. "The ravens cannot tell us from themselves."

You easily fly over the top of the cliff and alight softly on the ground. In just a few moments you feel that dizziness again, as you and the Wizard return to your true shapes.

To continue your adventure, turn to PAGE 24.

The entrance to the cave is so low that both of you must stoop to enter. Although it is dark inside, your eyes quickly adjust to the gloom. Steep stone steps leading upward are illuminated by an eerie greenish glow.

As you and your companion prepare to mount the steps, there is a sudden noise behind you. You whirl to see a giant shape blocking the entrance to the cave. It is the troll!

Although he is not as tall as you, he is wide and powerful, with a neck as thick as a tree trunk. You can see huge arm and shoulder muscles rippling under his hairy skin. His eyes are small and red, and his face reminds you of a nightmare. The troll opens his hideous mouth, revealing long, pointed fangs, and bellows, "Who dare to trespass in my cave?"

"The Wizard and the Warrior, who serve good King Henry," you reply boldly.

"Wizardry is powerless here!" the troll thunders. "Mad Morwenna's enchantment protects this cave. As for you, my fine Warrior, I see you carry an assortment of weapons. They will do you little good. In more than one thousand fights I've never been beaten. To be fair, I must warn you that I am a master swordsman. I advise you to forget your sword."

Go on to PAGE 20.

You size up the troll. He is perhaps the most powerful foe you have ever faced. But you have observed that he moves slowly. You doubt that such a heavy creature could have mastered swordplay.

On the other hand, you've learned that it is foolish to underestimate an opponent. The troll is certainly stronger than you and might be, as he claims, a skilled fighter. You consider your three other weapons. Speed may be your only advantage. Perhaps it's wisest to use a light weapon. Your thoughts immediately go to the lightest weapon of all — the Devil's Dagger.

If you've brought the Devil's Dagger, and trust it to defeat the troll, turn to PAGE 31.

If you do not have the Devil's Dagger, you must rely on the mighty Sword of the Golden Lion. Turn to PAGE 33.

Getting a stronger grip on your handhold in the rocky face of the cliff, you prepare to meet the ravens' attack. Whirling your weapon about you, you direct it at the vanguard of the flock. To your surprise, the weapon passes right through the attacking creatures, striking against the cliff. You brace for the pain of talons raking flesh, but it never comes.

"The ravens are not real," calls the Wizard below you. "Now that they are so near, I can sense that this illusion was created by sorcery. Whoever created the spell relied on it to frighten away any climbers." As soon as he has spoken, the flock of dark birds vanishes like mist.

Sheathing your weapon in relief, you resume your climb.

Go to PAGE 24.

Quickly, you draw your cloak around you and re-cite the words of the Shrink spell. Immediately there is a rush of wind, and when it has passed, the Cyclops has shrunk to the size of a chipmunk. His huge staff is now the size of a toothbrush, and his tiny eye blinks in surprise.

"What have you done to me?" the Cyclops squeaks. "What magic is this?"

"The magic of the Wizard of good King Henry!" answers the Warrior. He raises the Sword of the Golden Lion, and with one mighty blow strikes the Cyclops' head from its neck. Its body begins to roll down the trail, where it will join the bones of the countless others who have come before you.

You spend a few minutes tending to the Warrior's wounds. Then the two of you resume your climb.

To see what awaits you at the top of the cliff, turn to PAGE 34.

Now you and the Wizard are standing at the top of the cliff, facing the Haunted Castle of Raven-curse.

The castle is even more foreboding up close. Its barren grounds support only scrub brush and moss. The castle itself is so old it looks as if it might crumble to dust in a minute. A feeling of evil seeps from the dark, curtained windows — yet there is no movement, no sound.

The Wizard opens his belt pouch and withdraws the map. You study it together. (Look at pages 6 and 7.)

"There would seem to be two entrances only," you say.

"Let us examine both before we decide which to use," says your companion after a moment.

First, you and the Wizard approach the front door of the castle. It is twice as tall as a man and made of thick, sturdy wood. There is no doorknob — instead this door appears to open only from the inside. But there is a large iron knocker on the door, and below it a sign: ALL GUESTS MUST BE ANNOUNCED.

"I wonder who — or what — would answer a knock at this door?" you say with a shiver.

Go on to PAGE 25.

Now you and the Wizard circle to the back of the castle. If anything, it is even eerier than the front. The kitchen door is cloaked in shadows. On the windows, old wooden shutters hang loosely and bang in the wind. The smell of decay seems to rise from the walls. Somewhere in the distance you hear the cry of the ravens.

You turn to your wise friend. "Which do you think we should choose?" you ask.

Instead of answering, your companion closes his eyes a moment and concentrates. "I sense very powerful evil here," he says. "I must focus all my attention on it to prevent our falling under a spell. You make the choice of entrance, brave friend. I fear we will have our hands full, whichever the choice."

Which entrance do you choose?

If you choose to knock on the front door and see who answers, turn to PAGE 36.

If you'd rather take your chances on the kitchen door, go to PAGE 40.

26

You wait nervously, hoping against hope that the Warrior will soon reappear. You hold your cloak around you, ready to cast a spell.

After what seems a very long time (but is really only five minutes or so), a towering knight steps out from inside the dark castle. He is wearing heavy black armor, and on his gauntlet sits an evil-looking raven.

"Welcome to the Castle of Ravencurse," the Black Knight says. "Your friend, the Warrior, has received the customary greeting of Mad Morwenna. And now I must extend the same to you."

The raven rises into the air and begins to spin. It assumes the form of a whirlwind, and you realize that it is about to challenge your magic. You open your mouth to cast a spell, but before you can speak you find it impossible to move.

Too late, you realize that the strange statues around you were once human fighters, as you too used to be . . .

You hear the Black Knight laughing, and your heart is heavy — as heavy as the rest of you, which has turned to stone. Close the book now, and perhaps when you are in a lighter mood, you will return to the world of *Wizards, Warriors, and You.*

END

The flock of ravens is almost upon you. Their raucous cries split the air. Maintaining your grip on the cliff with one hand and both feet, you hold your chosen weapon, prepared to fight.

It would not be easy to fight even one attacker in this position. Fighting hundreds proves impossible. You begin to strike with your weapon as the ravens close in, but the weight of the weapon causes you to lose your balance, dragging the Wizard after you. As the ravens shriek in satisfaction, you and your companion fall to your deaths at the bottom of the cliff.

The Haunted Castle and its treasures still wait for adventurers brave enough to dare it. Will *you* dare to open this book again and return to the quest?

END

28

For a moment you hesitate, wondering if there is time to go for the Mace of the Mountain. But one look at the Wizard tells you he has not fully recovered from the blow. He wouldn't stand a chance against this knight. You may not have much of a chance either, without the aid of a weapon more powerful than your own. Yet you know you cannot leave your friend. Grasping your sword tightly, you consider your strategy.

"Defend yourself!" you call to the knight.

He turns, surprised. "What? You are not going after the Mace of the Mountain, puny one?"

"I will not leave my friend," you reply, "no matter what the consequences."

You brace yourself for the knight's attack, but instead he falls to his knees with a scream. "You've found the one weapon that can combat my evil." His voice is fading now and filled with disbelief. "Friendship and loyalty—who would have expected it from a puny warrior like you?" With that, he collapses. Cautiously, you approach, then lift his black visor. Inside, his rotting skull is disintegrating into dust, even as you watch.

There is a sudden loud sound, like a thunderclap, and for a moment everything goes dark. You feel a wind whistling about you, a sensation of heat, and then nothing. The darkness lifts.

Go on to PAGE 29.

To your astonishment, you are inside the castle. Next to you stands the Wizard, looking far stronger now. More of the strange stone statues line the castle's entrance hall.

"Thank you, my friend," says the Wizard.

"I think I have learned a valuable lesson," you reply as you return the Sword of the Golden Lion to its scabbard.

You both pause a moment to catch your breath, then exchange a glance. You know that it is time to resume your quest. What lies beyond the inner door of the entrance hall?

To enter that door, turn to PAGE 87.

The troll has drawn a heavy silver sword and holds it at his side. You can see that he is indeed a skilled swordsman. Slowly, you and the troll circle each other. As he moves close, you begin to doubt your choice of weapon. Will the Devil's Dagger be able to penetrate his thick hide?

Suddenly, the troll thrusts at you. Dodging his blow, you dart in and strike. Your dagger has found its mark. The troll howls with pain, green blood spurting from a shoulder wound. Enraged now, he thrusts again, missing completely.

The troll's reaction gives you the strategy you need. With lightning speed you strike again and again, wounding him slightly each time. The angrier the troll gets, the more clumsily he fights. Soon he is striking blindly, all trace of his skill gone.

Now you have only to wait for the opening. The troll swings wildly. Deftly, you step inside the arc of his sword and sink your dagger deep. For a moment it seems as if time stops. Then, with an inhuman howl, the troll crumples and lies in a pool of oozing green.

"Well fought, friend," says the Wizard softly.

With a shrug you retrieve the Devil's Dagger. "We've wasted enough time," you say. "Let's see where these stairs lead."

Turn to PAGE 24.

No sooner have you uttered the spell of Combat Magic than there is a bright flash of light and a clap of thunder. When they have died down you look around you, expecting to see Ravencurse Castle.

All you see is a blank wall behind you and, in front of you, an endless set of stone stairs leading downward.

Combat Magic has not worked. And you cannot use it again here.

You realize that Mad Morwenna has had the last laugh after all. Sadly, you and the Warrior resume your journey down the steps, knowing that you will never reach the . . .

END

As the Wizard watches from the stone steps, his magical powers contained by Morwenna's enchantment, you and the troll circle each other carefully. The troll has drawn a heavy silver sword that begins to glow brightly.

You raise the Sword of the Golden Lion and slash at the troll. He meets it easily with his glowing sword.

For many long moments the two of you battle, the troll easily sidestepping your thrusts. You realize that he is the best swordsman you have ever met.

Although you are strong and skilled, you are no match for the troll. Your arm begins to tire. Your moves are getting slower. Suddenly, the troll lunges forward and knocks your sword from your hand.

"Foolish human!" he cries, approaching you. "I warned you not to use a sword. Now prepare to die!"

You have fallen against the stone steps, near the Wizard. With an evil laugh, the troll approaches, his glowing sword held high. Your last thought before it strikes home is that you will never again doubt a troll's word.

You fought a brave battle, Warrior, but this quest has come to a close. Perhaps your next adventure will have a happier end, when next you enter the world of *Wizards, Warriors, and You*.

END

You are standing at the top of the cliff where a thick fog has settled. In front of you the Haunted Castle of Ravencurse looms through the mist. There is the unmistakable feel of evil in the air.

The Warrior draws his sword as the two of you approach. "Which entrance shall we use?" he asks.

You close your eyes and try to sense the evil forces that wait for you. It seems to you that the concentration of sorcery and evil is greatest at present in the back of the castle. You tell the Warrior your feelings.

"Then let us enter by the front," says the Warrior, boldly striding toward the main entrance. You are uneasy as you notice that the door is flanked by life-size statues of warriors and knights.

The front door begins to swing open with an unearthly creak. The Warrior has his sword ready, but no one emerges.

Cautiously, you approach the now-open door. Inside all is dark.

"I will go in," says the Warrior bravely. You watch as he steps inside and—vanishes!

Go on to PAGE 35.

There is no sound from the entrance hall. You wait a moment, but nothing happens.

Now you face a decision. Should you go into the dark hall after your friend? Or would it be wiser to wait until you have a clearer idea of the magic being used here?

If you decide to follow the Warrior inside, turn to PAGE 41.

If you think it is safer to wait for a few more minutes, turn to PAGE 26.

36

Looking more confident than you feel, you and the Wizard approach the huge front door. You notice that beside it are dozens of marble statues of knights and other fighters. You pull the knocker and let it hit the wood. THUD, THUD, THUD. For a moment nothing happens, and then you hear heavy footsteps behind the door.

The door creaks open.

"Who dares approach the Haunted Castle of Ravencurse?" says a deep, booming voice.

"Servants of King Henry," you answer.

The voice laughs. Then the door swings open. Before you is a tall knight, dressed in heavy black armor and carrying a gigantic mace.

You draw your sword protectively. Beside you the Wizard stands deep in concentration as he tries to sense the nature of the evil before you.

"Well, well," says the Black Knight. "The Warrior—and the Wizard. No matter. I am Sir Cynwyd of Ravencurse, and I will not let you pass."

The knight lifts his arm and without any warning swings the mace at the Wizard. To your horror, you see your friend fall to the ground, unconscious.

Go on to PAGE 38.

Again the knight swings, this time at you, but you dodge his blow. Sir Cynwyd chuckles as you raise your sword to block the next blow. With no effort at all, his mace sweeps the sword from your hand. Instantly, you draw another weapon and prepare to attack.

"Ordinary weapons are useless against me," the knight boasts. "Only the Mace of the Mountain, which is kept in the entrance hall, can help you. But it is far too powerful a weapon for such a puny warrior as you."

You know that your only chance is to try to get that mighty weapon. But to do so, you will have to leave the Wizard, who is now moaning on the ground beside you.

The Wizard sees your difficulty. "Go on, my friend," he says, his voice weak. "Don't worry about me."

The knight, too, sees your dilemma and begins to laugh. "Yes," he says, "by all means go search for the Mace of the Mountain. And when you return I will have only one of you to worry about."

The knight approaches the Wizard, his own mace held high. What do you do? Do you run into the entrance hall for the magic weapon? Or do you stay and try to defend the Wizard?

If you choose to stay, turn to PAGE 28.

If you decide to try for the Mace of the Mountain, go to PAGE 43.

You feel a moment of dizziness, as always, when you call up the Shift Shape spell. Then you feel your wings beating strongly. Beside you, the Warrior also soars.

You are starting to congratulate yourself on having found the best way to get to the top of the cliff when you are stopped in midair. You've flown into an area of magical turbulence. Just yards short of the edge of the cliff, Mad Morwenna's spell combats yours.

Though you concentrate all of your powers on breaking through Morwenna's magic, the wall of enchantment is overwhelming. Finally, you find a weakness in Mad Morwenna's spell, but before you can break it, Shift Shape wears off. And you and the Warrior return to your true forms—inches from the edge of the cliff.

Too bad, Wizard! Sorcery more powerful than yours has brought you down. Close the book quickly now, and perhaps, when your magic has restored itself, you will return to the Haunted Castle of Ravencurse.

END

While the Wizard continues to concentrate on the evil he senses, you draw your sword and approach the castle's kitchen door. You turn the knob, and to your surprise it comes off in your hand. A pile of rust falls to the stone steps below.

"This door has not been used in a very long time," you say.

The Wizard stands beside you as you push open the ancient wooden door. Its hinges creak with a sound like a thousand lost souls crying in the darkness. You and your friend step into the musty room.

The kitchen is huge, the size of King Henry's stables. There is a long wooden table at one end of the room. Its surface is covered with thick dust and cobwebs. An old-fashioned sink with a hand pump looks as if it has not been used for generations. Then you see what you've been looking for—the two other doors. From the map you know that one leads to the cellar and the other to the ballroom.

Now you must decide which treasure to go after first.

If you want to go to the cellar and seek the Crimson Crown of Ravencurse, turn to PAGE 49.

If you decide to go after the Bottomless Basket first, go to the ballroom on PAGE 87.

You know that the Warrior is in great danger and that you must move quickly. You take a deep breath, then step inside the castle door. The blackness is so complete, you realize that it could only have been created by a spell. You call for your friend, but there is no answer.

Suddenly, a greenish glow appears. In the glow you can see the dim figure of a knight.

"Welcome to Ravencurse," says the knight in an eerie, hollow voice. "We did not invite you to come, but now that you are here, we invite you to stay—forever."

"Where is my friend, the Warrior?" you demand angrily.

"He is where he will cause no more trouble for Mad Morwenna," answers the knight.

Before you can ask the knight what he means, he vanishes into the darkness. In the next instant the door to the ballroom opens.

You step into the ballroom cautiously, looking for the Warrior. At first all you see is crumbling furniture and dusty tapestries hanging on the walls. But then you notice a gigantic spider's web, extending from floor to ceiling, covering an entire side of the room.

Go on to PAGE 42.

42

At the top of the web is a huge spider, shimmering black and silver. Behind the web you can see the Bottomless Basket gleaming. And now you see something that makes your blood run cold. Wrapped in silk from head to toe, and dangling helplessly from a corner of the web, is the Warrior!

As you approach the web, the spider moves toward you menacingly. Quickly you review your spells. You decide that your best chance rests on first putting the spider to sleep. Then you can call on either The Wind, to blow the web away, or Merlin's Fire, to burn the web. You know that there is risk with any of these powerful spells and you are worried about depleting your powers, but you have no choice.

The spider reaches out with its hairy legs to grab you. The web is vibrating like a taut bowstring. Quickly, you pull your cloak around you and chant the hypnotic words of Sorcerer's Sleep. The spider shudders all over, then its legs droop, and it stops moving.

Quickly now, choose one of the other two spells and say the words as fast as you can.

If you have chosen The Wind, turn to **PAGE 60**.
If you prefer to trust Merlin's Fire, go to **PAGE 48**.

With a last glance at the Wizard and the Black Knight, you hurry into the castle. Quickly you spot the Mace of the Mountain, hidden in a niche high in the wall. You must stand on tiptoe to reach it, and when you do, you discover that it is almost too heavy to lift.

Worried about the safety of your friend, you tug with all your might. At last the Mace begins to loosen. You must hurry. The sounds of struggle outside give you the power you need to pull the weapon from its holder. It takes all of your strength to hold it aloft. Then you quickly go back out.

The door is blocked by the huge figure of Sir Cynwyd. You cannot see the Wizard, and you cannot hear anything.

The knight lifts his own mace and prepares to strike. You do the same. "You haven't a chance," says the knight. "You may hold the Mace of the Mountain, but you haven't the strength to wield it. Give up now and it will be over quickly."

In answer you lift the Mace and swing. You realize that this may be the most difficult battle of your life. What will be the outcome of the fight?

Flip a coin seven times. If there are more heads than tails, turn to PAGE 67.

If there are more tails than heads, turn to PAGE 57.

The zombie and the raven look surprised as the Wizard vanishes, and they don't see the black shape that swoops up toward the ceiling.

"*Eeeeaaiii!*" wails the raven, sounding less menacing.

The zombie starts to approach you, but before it can move, you raise your weapon and strike down the raven. The bird utters a last shriek and falls from its master's shoulder, dying.

"You'll pay for this!" vows the zombie. With a roar of rage, it grabs for you.

You step aside easily. Out of the corner of your eye you see the Wizard, in raven form, lifting the crown from its perch on the shelf.

Again the zombie tries to attack you, and again you step aside. You realize you cannot kill the creature, and you know it will not give up. With a mighty blow, you attack the zombie's legs. It goes down on the cellar floor. Before it can begin to heal itself and attack again, you are on your way up the stairs.

A moment later, the Wizard stands beside you in his true form, triumphantly holding the Crimson Crown.

Congratulations! You have won one of the treasures of the Castle of Ravencurse.

If you have not yet won the Bottomless Basket, go to **PAGE 87**.

If you now have both treasures, it is time to escape from the castle. Quick! Turn to **PAGE 68**.

You are so weak that you can't tell if the spell has worked, until you hear the THUNK of an arrow hitting the Invisible Shield.

Instantly, the Warrior realizes what you have done and stops shooting, looking puzzled.

Now the spider surprises you. It climbs down the web and sets you gently on the ground.

"Even though you meant only to save your own life," it says, "you saved my own at the same time. I can't kill you after that. Be still a while and the venom will wear off."

You are beginning to feel stronger by the minute.

"What about the Bottomless Basket?" the Warrior asks.

"Take it," says the spider. "I am getting tired of guarding it. But I don't think you'll take it far. Mad Morwenna is not likely to let you leave this castle alive."

In a few minutes you have regained your strength. You and the Warrior now have one of the two treasures. Next you must try to get the Crimson Crown of Ravencurse. Will the spider prove right? Or will you be able to get the other treasure and escape from Ravencurse Castle?

To find out, turn to PAGE 50.

46

While the Warrior chooses the two strongest weapons he has, you draw your cloak around yourself and prepare to recite the spell of Visions.

The plan is for the Warrior to hold off the zombies while you take the Crimson Crown from Rudolf's head. You are relying on the magic to keep the zombies so confused that they won't be able to hurt you.

You just hope that the spell works correctly.

To find out what happens after you have finished reciting your spell, flip a coin.

If it comes up heads, turn to PAGE 56.
If it is tails, go to PAGE 75.

The Warrior draws his weapon, holding the zombies back. At the same time you pull your cloak around you and recite the spell of Sorcerer's Sleep.

Rudolf, king of the zombies, is moving toward you. His sharp, pointed teeth are grinning in anticipation of their next meal.

There is a sudden rush of wind. The zombies stop and look at one another, then slowly sink to the floor, asleep.

"Keep your weapon ready," you say to your companion. "The length of time this spell will last is unpredictable."

The Warrior stands guard as you approach the sleeping form of Rudolf of Ravencurse. You start to slip the Crimson Crown from the zombie's head.

There is a sudden noise.

To find out what the noise is:

If you are reading this book any time from 3 P.M. until midnight, turn to PAGE 74.

If you are reading it between midnight and 3 P.M., turn to PAGE 61.

Merlin's Fire begins to glow and sparkle. Soon the entire web is ablaze. You see that the silken threads wrapping the Warrior are rapidly burning off. Freed, he jumps down to the floor while you dash behind the web to retrieve the Bottomless Basket.

At that moment your spells wear off. The fire stops burning and the spider wakes.

"What have you done?" it cries in anguish. "You have destroyed my web!" Before you can move, the spider attacks, biting your arm. Then it quickly climbs up one of the unburned strands, carrying you with it. The spider's venom makes you feel weak all over. You try to call out to the Warrior, but all you can manage is a whisper.

"Let my friend go or you will be sorry!" shouts the Warrior from far below.

"Your friend is the one who will be sorry," the spider replies. "I am an enchanted Spider of Doom!"

You feel a chill go through you. From your magical studies, you know that anything that happens to a Spider of Doom also happens to any person the spider touches. Unfortunately, the Warrior doesn't know this. You see him fitting a poisoned arrow to his longbow.

Somehow you must warn him.

Quick! Turn to PAGE 13!

You are standing at the top of the cellar stairs with the Wizard right behind you. Your hand on your sword, you begin to descend. The stairway is completely dark, the cellar even darker. At the bottom you stand for a moment, waiting for your eyes to adjust to the dimness.

Gradually, you are able to see that the cellar is empty—or nearly empty. On a stone shelf high above you rests the one source of light, a glowing red crown.

Before you can figure out how to get the crown, you hear a hideous cawing. Walking toward you is a creature dressed in rags. And on its shoulder sits a red-eyed raven.

"I have been waiting for you," the creature says slowly. "I am king of the zombies and guardian of the Crimson Crown."

"*Eeeeaaiiiii!*" the raven screams. It is like the wail of someone dying.

The zombie leers at you and says, "When the raven has screamed three times it will attack. Take your last look at the Crimson Crown you die for. No one, Warrior, survives the raven's poisoned talons."

Go to PAGE 85.

50

Cautiously, you and the Warrior enter the kitchen. There is an old sink and a rotting wooden table, but nothing that appears dangerous—at the moment.

The cellar door is open, and flickering torches set in the wall light the way down. Clearly, you are expected.

You feel a strong sense of evil, yet you do not hesitate. Both of you know that you must find the hidden treasure — the Crimson Crown of Ravencurse. You are prepared to meet any foe in this castle.

With the Warrior behind you, his hand on his sword, you lead the way down the dusty steps. Somewhere you hear water dripping. There is a faint sound of music and laughter. You feel a deep sense of unease.

To find out what is waiting for you at the bottom of the stairs, turn to PAGE 70.

"An excellent guess!" says the spider. "I am glad to let you go. I wish you luck in your dealings with Mad Morwenna."

Quickly, the spider unwraps you. You take the basket and begin to move back through the web toward the Wizard. There is a sudden shriek, and you look up to see the spider being attacked by a raven as big as it is.

"This is how traitors to Mad Morwenna die!" cries the raven. The spider struggles, but within moments the raven has ripped it apart. "You are next!" it screams.

You have almost reached the edge of the web when the raven begins to dive for you. "Throw me a weapon!" you call to the Wizard.

"Which one?" he calls back.

If you ask him to throw you the longbow, the morning star, the crossbow, or the battle-axe, turn to PAGE 82.

If you ask him to throw you any other weapon, turn to PAGE 64.

52

You and the Warrior set the Crimson Crown and the Bottomless Basket down on the step below you. Instantly, they vanish.

The shadowy form of Mad Morwenna ripples and twists; then it, too, disappears. The last you hear of her is a ghostly laugh.

"This is a desperate situation," you say. "And it calls for desperate measures. The only spell that has a chance of working is Combat Magic. But it requires great strength, and my powers are drained. Be ready for anything, my brave friend."

You draw your cloak around you and wearily begin to pronounce the words to this most potent spell. You are acutely aware of your fatigue, and though the Warrior stands with his weapons ready, you know that everything depends on how much power you have left.

To discover the outcome of your spell, toss a coin until it comes up heads.

If it comes up heads on the first, second, or third try, turn to PAGE 79.

If it comes up heads on the fourth try or later, go to PAGE 32.

As the wolf charges the Warrior, its two heads snapping viciously, you quickly draw your cloak around you and begin to chant the words for the Shrink spell. You are aware of your waning power and hope that the spell will work correctly.

There is a brief flash of light, which tells you that the spell has worked. But it has worked on the Warrior instead of the wolf! Suddenly, your friend is the size of a mouse!

Snarling, the wolf pounces on the Warrior and gobbles him down in one bite. It licks its muzzles in satisfaction, then turns to you.

"Your friend was a delicious morsel," the beast growls. "And now for the meal."

The failure of the Shrink spell proves that your powers are too weak to help you anymore.

Before the wolf can get any closer, you would do well to close this book. You have used your magic well, Wizard, but even the most powerful magic can sometimes be overcome.

Open the book only when you feel strong enough to again brave the evils of the Haunted Castle of Ravencurse.

END

54

Even though you want to help, you realize that any spell you cast now might backfire. Helplessly, you watch as the Warrior continues to battle the two-headed wolf. The beast is much quicker than your friend, but the Warrior is an excellent fighter.

With his new weapon, the Warrior blinds the smaller head. The wolf screams with pain and rage. In its fury, the wolf knocks the Warrior to the ground. Again you think of trying a spell. The beast moves in for the kill. Suddenly, the Warrior pulls the Devil's Dagger from his belt. As the larger head reaches down to tear out your friend's throat, the Warrior suddenly plunges the dagger into the wolf's chest. There is a great fountain of blood, and the beast topples over. The Warrior has won!

You help your friend to stand. He is exhausted, but you can see that his injuries are not serious. Though both of you are weakened, you know you must get away from the castle as quickly as possible.

The back door is still glowing with Morwenna's Shield.

You must try to exit by the front door.

Turn to PAGE 69 to see what happens next.

You hear the Wizard murmuring his Shift Shape incantation, but you are too busy to listen. You must choose a weapon to fight off the evil zombie and raven. Remember that a zombie is neither dead nor alive and cannot be killed. It can only be injured.

While the Wizard, now in raven form, is attempting to get the Crimson Crown, you approach your foes, the weapon of your choice raised, ready to strike.

The raven screams and swoops toward you as the zombie approaches.

In the small cellar, the battle-axe, the flail, or the Devil's Dagger would be the most effective weapons. If you have brought any of these, turn to PAGE 44.

If you have not brought one of these, you still have a chance—though a desperate one—using the Sword of the Golden Lion. But which foe should you fight first?

If you decide to fight the raven first, go to PAGE 72.

If you decide instead to try to disable the zombie, go to PAGE 80.

The instant that you have finished reciting the spell of Visions, the air is split by a shriek from Rudolf.

"Help!" he cries. "A dragon!"

Then the other zombies begin screaming. Moments later, they are running away from each other and into the walls, screaming about trolls and mummies and poisonous bats. They are so confused they don't remember that they cannot be killed.

Still, you must stay on guard. The Warrior strikes out at the zombies with his weapons. Soon, several of them are stunned, and there is more room to maneuver in the cellar. Now the Warrior approaches Rudolf, who is cowering in a corner, still screaming about a dragon. Swiftly, your friend strikes the zombie's head from his shoulders. Rudolf's body, still confused, begins to run in the opposite direction. You know it will be several minutes before he is able to recover the head. Quickly, you take the Crimson Crown from it, then you and the Warrior climb the stairs back to the kitchen. You shut the door behind you with a sigh of relief.

Then you plan your next move—escape!

Since you are already in the kitchen, you may prefer to try to escape by the back door. If so, go to PAGE 83.

If you think it is safer to use a door you have already tried, go back to the front door, on PAGE 69.

Your arms trembling, you lift the heavy Mace of the Mountain. The evil Sir Cynwyd towers above you, his own mace ready to strike you down.

You edge around him and out the door. Then you begin to back down the path that leads to the cliff.

"Coward!" calls the knight. "Are you afraid of me, then?"

You don't answer but continue to move closer and closer to the edge of the cliff.

"Stand and fight!" cries the knight.

You are now at the edge of the cliff. The knight towers above you. Now you raise the Mace and strike at your foe's knees. With a howl, he begins to topple over. His heavy armor makes it hard for him to get up. Before he can recover, you push him toward the cliff. You stand and watch as the Black Knight rolls over the edge, screaming and cursing King Henry.

Now you run back to the castle door. You are relieved to see the Wizard sitting up, looking almost himself.

"I could have summoned enough power to create one spell," he says, sounding tired. "But I do not think my magic would have lasted long. I am glad of your strength, my friend. Now, shall we enter the castle and see what further adventures await us?"

You agree. Together you enter the castle.

Ahead of you is the door to the ballroom. To find out what is on the other side, turn to PAGE 87.

58

Carefully you make your way through the sticky silk, parting it like a curtain, climbing over the thickest strands. At the same time the spider moves toward you, its fangs dripping venom. Suddenly it reaches out with two of its eight hairy legs. Before you can move, it has grabbed you. You struggle, but the spider overpowers you, pinning your arms to your side with its silk. "Who are you and why have you come here?" it demands.

You answer truthfully, "We are the Warrior and Wizard of good King Henry, sent to take the treasures in this castle."

"You would make a nice dinner for me," says the spider. "But I have no love for Mad Morwenna. Before she enchanted me I was a master weaver. I made all of the tapestries you see here. I will offer you a chance. If you can guess how many eggs I have in my egg sac, I will let you go."

You look upward to where a shimmering ball of silk holds the spider's eggs. It is impossible to see from here how many there are.

"How many eggs do I have?" taunts the spider. "Guess now."

You look out at the Wizard, but he cannot help you. You take a deep breath and make the best guess you can.

If you guessed more than 20 eggs, go to **PAGE 62**.
If you guessed 11 to 20 eggs, go to **PAGE 73**.
If you guessed 1 to 10 eggs, go to **PAGE 51**.

There is a loud, rushing sound, like a hundred tornadoes at once. The Wind spell has worked!

The ballroom furniture crashes against the walls. The tapestries whirl through the air like flying carpets. As you watch, the spider's web is torn into a million tiny pieces. The silk threads trapping the Warrior are blown off, and he jumps lightly to the ground.

The spider, which has curled itself into a ball, is blown upward, into a corner of the ceiling. Before it can move, the Warrior quickly runs to where the web once was and takes the Bottomless Basket.

The wind dies down, and you look at each other in triumph. You now have one of the treasures of the Castle of Ravencurse. And you are both alive and well.

You take a deep breath, knowing that you must next go to the cellar to seek the Crimson Crown. And after that, you will still have to escape.

But one step at a time, clever Wizard. Turn to PAGE 50 to enter the kitchen and begin your journey into the cellar.

The noise you heard was only the sound of a zombie snoring, which is loud and disgusting, but harmless.

Moving swiftly, you remove the Crimson Crown from the sleeping zombie's head and place it on your own. With the Warrior's weapon still ready, the two of you quickly climb the stairway back to the kitchen. Below you the zombies sleep on.

Congratulations! You now have both of the treasures of the Haunted Castle of Ravencurse.

Now all that remains is for you to escape. You must decide whether to try to leave through the front door or the back.

If you decide to try to escape by the back door, turn to PAGE 83.

If you prefer to take your chances at the front door, go to PAGE 69.

"More than twenty?" says the spider with a laugh. "My nest has never been that full. Perhaps my next visitor will be a better judge than you."

You are about to say something, but suddenly your mouth is full of sticky gray silk as the spider finishes wrapping you up. You, too, hope that the next person brave enough to try the web will be a better guesser than you.

You don't really want to know what the spider does to you next. So close the book, and when you're ready to weave a new web of adventure, return to the world of *Wizards, Warriors, and You.*

END

Alas, just as the raven flies within range of your sword, the spell of Invisibility wears off. The raven swerves and dives, and you feel its claws raking your back. Then you feel no more.

Your fight has been brave, Warrior, but it has come to an end. Now, if there is still breath in you, concentrate on the powers of recovery you've been taught. Know that no one before you has survived the raven's talons. But, perhaps, if your healing skills are strong enough and your heart brave enough, you will again dare the Haunted Castle of Ravencurse.

END

64

You catch the weapon and turn quickly, prepared to meet the raven's attack. It dives at you and you swing, but miss. Again the raven dives, reaching out with its long talons. Then you get an idea. You move back into the tattered strands of the web. They are not strong, but there are thousands of them, and they *are* sticky. Maybe they'll slow the raven down.

Enraged, the bird dives again. Its talons entangle themselves in the web for just a moment, but long enough to give you your chance. Moving quickly, you strike at the bird with your weapon. You hear it shriek. You have wounded one of its wings. The raven tries to soar to the ceiling again, but the wing flaps uselessly at its side.

Now you close in for the kill. With one mighty blow, you put the raven out of its misery.

Congratulations, Warrior. You have gained one of the two treasures of Ravencurse.

If you also have the Crimson Crown, turn to PAGE 68.

If you have not yet won the Crimson Crown, you must go to the cellar, on PAGE 49.

"We will not give up these treasures," you say boldly to the ghostly figure. You keep tight hold of the basket while the Wizard steadies the crown on his head.

"Then you will give up your lives!" Morwenna says. There is a sudden clap of thunder and a searing smell of smoke. The wind whistles by you, and suddenly, you find yourself back in the kitchen of the castle.

To see what is waiting for you there, go to PAGE 90.

"We are glad to see you," Rudolf continues. "No one new has come to our party in quite a while."

You feel your blood run cold. You know that Rudolf lived 500 years ago, and that zombies are neither living nor dead. Creatures of darkness, they feed on human flesh. Anyone defeated by a zombie becomes one.

"The Crimson Crown is guarded well," you tell the Warrior. "It will take my strongest magic and all your skill to defeat these evil creatures."

Your friend agrees. Since zombies cannot be killed, your only hope is to confuse or outwit them. The zombies start to move toward you slowly. Quickly, you and the Warrior confer. You decide on a combination of magic and weaponry to give you the best chance against these loathsome creatures.

If you choose the combination of Visions and two of the Warrior's weapons, turn to PAGE 46.

If you choose instead to use one weapon along with the Sorcerer's Sleep, turn to PAGE 47.

The Mace of the Mountain is clearly a weapon of magic. As you swing, it seems to become lighter, and it strikes a mighty blow against Sir Cynwyd's armor.

"A good thrust," says the knight, "but not good enough. In the right hands this weapon can overpower even me. But you are no longer as strong as you were, for your friend the Wizard is no more."

As he speaks you suddenly realize that your strength is failing. You look down to see your friend, the Wizard, lying in a pool of blood, and sadness fills you. Still, you struggle to lift the heavy weapon one more time, but Sir Cynwyd moves before you do. You do not feel a thing as the evil knight's mace splits your skull in two.

Warrior, this adventure has not turned out as you planned. You and the Wizard now join the ghosts of Ravencurse, doomed to haunt the castle until its evil is broken.

END

With one hand on your sword and the other holding the Bottomless Basket, you lead the way to the entrance hall. There, a tall figure dressed in shimmering black robes stands before the door. The figure turns and smiles, revealing white, pointed teeth. From her long, dark hair and beautiful features, you know that this must be Mad Morwenna.

"So we meet at last," she says. "Did you really think I would let you take my treasures?"

You lift your sword. "Stand aside," you say.

The ghost of Mad Morwenna only laughs. "Don't be silly," she chides. "I have nothing to fear from you. Or you," she adds, turning to the Wizard. "Don't make me use force. Drop the treasures here, and I will let you continue. If you do not give them up now, a death of unimaginable pain awaits you."

Go to PAGE 86.

You have almost completed this perilous quest. Now you and the Warrior leave the kitchen, hurry through the ballroom, and into the entrance hall.

Then you stop. The castle's front door is gone! In its place are stairs, leading downward. Above the stairs are these words: THIS WAY OUT.

"It must be a trick," the Warrior says.

"Nothing in this castle is what it seems," you agree. "But we seem to have little choice."

The stairway is unusually steep. Although there are torches lighting the way, it is difficult to see. Strange shadows dance along the stone walls, as if alive. You realize that the stairs must lead down through the steep cliff. You expect the bottom to appear soon, but the steps keep going down, down, down. Each step seems much steeper than the last.

"Powerful sorcery is at work here," you mutter.

It feels as if the stairway will never end. Both you and the Warrior are beginning to tire. You look behind you and are startled to see a solid wall. The steps behind you have disappeared! Before you have time to worry about this new difficulty, a high voice shrieks in the darkness below.

Go to PAGE 88

The cellar of Ravencurse Castle is dark and damp, reeking of decay. The faint music has faded away.

Staying close together, you and the Warrior look around. There are dozens of human-sized shapes against the walls, each covered with a dusty cloth. You see nothing else.

"The Crimson Crown must be under one of these cloths," says the Warrior. He starts to move toward them, but you raise your hand to stop him.

At that moment one of the shapes suddenly moves. Throwing off its covering, it stands. It is shaped like a man, but more hideous than any man you have ever seen. Although dressed in fine silk clothing, its flesh is rotting, exposing parts of its skeleton. On its head is a golden crown, set thickly with blood-red rubies.

"Welcome to Mad Morwenna's party," the figure says in a hollow voice. "I am Rudolf of Ravencurse, now king of the zombies. And these"— he spreads his hands—"are my friends."

The other shapes begin to move, throwing off their coverings. They stand up, stretching and yawning, dressed in rags that were once beautiful suits and gowns. Each one is as grisly as Rudolf, their king. The ghostly music begins again.

Go to PAGE 66.

The Warrior leads the way as the two of you begin to pick your way up the sheer face of the cliff. This would be a difficult climb even for an experienced mountaineer. The wind and the circling gulls keep you company as the ground drops farther and farther away. Though you and your companion are both in good shape, you are exhausted before you have climbed halfway to the top.

Suddenly, your way is blocked by sharp metal spikes projecting downward. You realize that it will be impossible to climb around them.

You think quickly. Knowing you must conserve your strength, you decide to turn yourself and your companion into seagulls.

You tell the Warrior what you plan to do, then you hold on tightly to a root growing out of the cliff. With your other hand you pull your cloak around you and murmur the words for the Shift Shape spell.

To discover the outcome of this spell:

If you are reading this on a Tuesday, Thursday, or Saturday, turn to PAGE 30.

If you are reading it on a Monday, Wednesday, Friday, or Sunday, turn to PAGE 39.

72

Although the raven is a small target, difficult to hit, desperation gives you strength and skill you did not know you possessed.

The bird screams for the third time and dives. As the raven speeds toward you, you meet it with your sword. It shrieks as you cut it in half. Black feathers flutter to the ground.

You hear an inhuman bellow and turn to meet the zombie.

"You have killed my raven!" it moans.

"And you are next!" you cry. You lift your sword and, with one mighty blow, strike the zombie's head off. Its body sways, then topples, and lies on the floor, blindly groping about for its head.

Above you, you hear a caw of triumph and look up to see the Wizard carrying the Crimson Crown in his raven's beak. He alights at your feet and resumes his true shape.

"We have won one of the two treasures of Ravencurse," says the Wizard.

The two of you quickly go back up the stairs, prepared for the next step of your adventure.

If you have also won the Bottomless Basket, go to PAGE 68.

If you have not, you must proceed to the ballroom on PAGE 87.

"Sorry," says the spider. "There are fewer eggs than that. Now be still, Warrior." The spider's legs dart in and out, binding you. Desperately you struggle, but it's useless.

You look through the web for a last glance at your friend. The Wizard has wrapped himself in his cloak. You know he's risking his life, trying to counter this powerful magic with his own. There must be something you can do. What was it he said—something about the magic being so focused that only cunning could work against it? You realize that strategy, not force, is your only hope. And maybe a strategy that will work is a distraction— something to *un*focus the spider's power.

"We can help you against Morwenna," you say to the spider.

For an instant the spider stops spinning and regards you with curiosity. That instant is all the Wizard needs.

Go to PAGE 89.

You relax as you realize that the noise you heard was just the sound of the zombie king snoring. Again you reach for the Crimson Crown. Unfortunately, you're a little too relaxed. Without warning, the zombie king wakes, reaches past you, and grabs your friend. Before you can even cry out, Rudolf breaks the Warrior's neck with one clean snap.

Quickly, you draw your cloak around you to recite a spell—any spell! But the zombies are too fast. Dozens of them surround you, grinning horribly. They pull your cloak from your shoulders, and soon you, too, clever Wizard, have joined their endless party in the Haunted Castle of Ravencurse.

To return to the castle in human form, open the book and begin again.

END

You know the exact moment when the spell takes effect — because at that instant King Henry seems to appear in the cellar, riding a large blue butterfly.

The spell of Visions has backfired, affecting you and the Warrior instead of the zombies.

"Be careful, friend," you warn the Warrior. "Escape if you can!"

But that is impossible for both of you. All around you are hundreds of butterflies. You know that some of them are really zombies. You cannot find the stairway to safety, because the entire cellar has now been transformed into a large, grassy meadow.

It is a warm, sunny day. You are so confused by that vision that you do not even notice the moment when you, too, are transformed into a zombie.

Alas, this adventure in the Haunted Castle has come to an end. But the next time you open this book, you will surely have better luck . . . or will you?

END

"Very well," you say to Mad Morwenna. "We accept your terms." The Wizard sets the Crimson Crown on the ground a few feet in front of her.

"What about the Bottomless Basket?" she demands.

"Here it is!" you cry. With one mighty motion, you throw the priceless object directly at her. Although a ghost, Morwenna ducks, and in that instant the Wizard draws his cloak around him.

"Fools!" she cries. "The only chance you had was to keep the treasures! It is from them that I draw my power!"

Before your friend can finish his incantation, Mad Morwenna waves her ghostly hands. There is a mighty flash of lightning and a deafening roar. When it is over, the Wizard has been turned into a statue of stone, his cloak drawn around him forever, his mouth open in a word he will never finish.

You see all this because you are facing the Wizard—permanently. You, too, have been turned to stone. Sadly, you realize that the Wizard and the Warrior have joined the marble guardians of the Haunted Castle of Ravencurse.

END

The Wizard draws his cloak around him and mutters the incantation for his spell. Suddenly, he disappears. You look down at your arm and grin. It's not there, either, but you can feel the comforting weight of the Sword of the Golden Lion in your hand.

Raising your sword, you approach the zombie, who is looking around in confusion. "What manner of magic is this?" he demands.

"The magic of good King Henry's Wizard!" you cry. With a mighty lunge, you strike the zombie's head from its shoulders.

The raven flies up in the air, screeching. Holding your sword ready, you wait for its attack. The bird can't see you, but it must be able to sense you. Flying in great arcs, it swoops nearer and nearer.

"*Eeeeeaaiii!*" the raven screams for the third time and hurtles toward you.

Turn to PAGE 63.

"There is no reason for us to trust you," the Warrior says to the spirit.

"Then prepare to die!" Mad Morwenna answers. "You now have ten seconds."

You can see that the ghost means business. Although you do not know what she has in mind, you decide to create the Invisible Shield, just in case.

"In five seconds you will vanish from the face of the earth!" hisses Mad Morwenna.

You draw your cloak around you. Quickly, you say the words to the Invisible Shield spell.

"Now!" cries the ghost, and at that instant you finish reciting your spell. The air crackles with colored sparks. Your spell and Mad Morwenna's have been cast at the same moment. Only one of them will prove effective.

Too late, you wish that you had used a stronger spell. The colored sparks continue to dance around you, and then there is a bright flash of lightning as Morwenna's Disappearance spell claims you and your friend.

Alas, Wizard, this quest has come to an end. You no longer exist in the Haunted Castle of Ravencurse—or anywhere else. But if you can close this book and then open it again, you can return to match your magic against Mad Morwenna and her evil servants.

END

There is an ear-splitting roar, and the wind begins to whistle around you. The wind grows stronger, and soon it has become a whirlwind. It lifts you and the Warrior and carries you, up, up, up.

The noise is deafening. And now the light begins to grow brighter, flickering on and off. Suddenly, the noise stops. The wind sets you gently down. You look around. You and the Warrior are standing on the ground. Above you is a clear blue sky. In front of you lie the Crimson Crown and the Bottomless Basket.

Stunned, you look around for Ravencurse Castle. But all you can see is rubble. You turn to look at the Warrior. He looks shocked; he seems more exhausted than you have ever seen him. You know exactly how he feels.

"The spell worked," you say quietly. "Better than I had even hoped. All here was enchantment, and now the spell is broken. The castle and everything in it—including Mad Morwenna herself—are no more."

You pick up the treasures and turn your back on the rubble. Slowly, you and the Warrior begin the long journey home.

For King Henry's greeting to you, turn to **PAGE 93**.

As the griffins lie dying around you, you look to see how the Wizard is doing in his battle with Mad Morwenna. Where the Wizard and Morwenna stood, bright flames are leaping and spreading throughout the room.

You run toward the fire to rescue your companion, then you hear his cry behind you. "We must get out—quickly!"

Holding tightly to the Bottomless Basket, you follow the Wizard out the back door. Behind you, the shrieks of Mad Morwenna seem to pierce the castle walls.

"What happened to her?" you ask your friend.

"Morwenna weakened herself trying to call up the Spell of the Vipers," says the Wizard. "In that instant I invoked Shift Shape and turned her into a wooden table. Then I set the table ablaze with Merlin's Fire."

For several more minutes you and the Wizard watch as the fire spreads throughout the castle, destroying it and all of its evil. Then, holding tightly to your treasures, you turn and set off for home and good King Henry.

For his welcome, turn to PAGE 93.

The giant raven dives. You wield your weapon, prepared to meet its attack. But your weapon is heavy, and the raven zooms in behind you. Too late, you see what it is after: not you, but the Bottomless Basket of Ravencurse.

Shrieking in satisfaction, the raven snatches the basket and flies toward the ceiling. It turns the basket upside down, and gold and jewels begin to fall out, as thickly and heavily as rain.

"Run!" you call to the Wizard, but at that moment you see him go down, hit by a heavy diamond. For a while, you dodge the missiles, but there are too many of them. Soon the room is waist-deep in treasure, and you can hardly move. You never thought that you would have more treasure than you wanted, but, alas, this has come to pass.

The raven drops a ruby the size of a pumpkin directly above your head. Close the book quickly before the ruby lands. And the next time you feel in the mood for adventure, open the book and return again to the Haunted Castle of Ravencurse.

END

The castle's back door is old and crumbling, its hinges rusted nearly through. It is apparent that no one has used it in a very long time. The Warrior places his hand on the knob. Suddenly there is a brilliant flash of light, knocking him to the ground. Standing over the Warrior is a gray timber wolf with two huge heads. Each of its mouths is filled with sharp, glittering teeth.

"You have set up Morwenna's Shield!" roars the larger head. "Nobody exits through this door! Prepare to meet your doom!"

You are still exhausted from the number of spells you have recently cast. Noticing your fatigue, the Warrior calls out reassuringly, "Don't worry about me, friend. I'm not afraid of a wolf—even one with two heads!"

Turn to PAGE 84.

The Warrior strikes at the wolf with his sword, slashing its hairy chest. Enraged, the wolf, its jaws snapping, leaps at your friend. It knocks the sword from his hand. Immediately, the Warrior draws another weapon.

You face a dilemma. If you try to cast a spell now, you will use up your remaining power. And Mad Morwenna may have more surprises in store for you. But if you don't, the wolf may destroy the Warrior.

If you decide to help the Warrior, go to PAGE 53.

If you prefer to trust your friend's skill and courage, go to PAGE 54.

Quickly, you turn to the Wizard. "I will need your help," you whisper. "If you can change yourself into a raven and steal the Crimson Crown, I will fight these creatures."

"That fight is far too dangerous, my friend. Let me try a spell of Invisibility, and perhaps we will both escape."

"*Eeeeaaiiiii!*" the raven screams.

"Which is it to be?" the Wizard asks.

If you decide to let the Wizard make you invisible, turn to PAGE 77.

If you think you can defeat the raven and the zombie, turn to PAGE 55.

In whispers, you and the Wizard confer. "I'm afraid Morwenna is best fought with magic," says the Wizard. "If we pretend to give up the treasure, I may be able to cast a spell over her. It's a very long chance indeed, and if you agree to it, I'll need your help."

You know that weapons will not do much good against a ghost, but you're reluctant to even pretend to give up the treasures you've fought so hard for. Something tells you that giving in to Morwenna could be deadly.

Should you trust your instincts or the wise counsel of your friend?

If you pretend to give up the treasures and try to fight Mad Morwenna, turn to PAGE 76.

If you prefer to hold the treasures and see what happens, go on to PAGE 65.

You look around in wonder. You are in the ball-room of Ravencurse Castle. High windows reach to the ceiling. On three sides of the room beautiful tapestries, depicting hunting scenes and banquets, hang from the walls. But the fourth side of the room is hidden, completely covered by what seems to be a gray fog.

With sword drawn, you cross to that side of the room. As you near it you realize that the fog is made of millions of tiny strands of gray silk, exactly like . . .

"A spider's web!" you and the Wizard say to-gether. Without touching it, the two of you peer through the thick, sticky strands. In one corner, behind the web, sits a basket of woven gold. And directly above the basket hangs a shimmering black spider, as big as a man. The spider watches you with glowing red eyes.

Go on to PAGE 94.

Now the shadows swirl in front of you, and suddenly they come together, forming one tall, slender figure. The figure doesn't seem to have a face, but speaks from a hollow point where its mouth should be. You realize that it is speaking in rhyme:

> *Now Mad Morwenna brings her curse:*
> *Those who come here will die or worse!*
> *You who steal the Basket and Crown*
> *Will find that you can travel only down.*

The ghostly figure begins to laugh maniacally. Although it is still in shadow, you can see that its face is that of a beautiful woman. It must be Morwenna!

"Greetings, my friends," says the ghost. "Your courage and magic have served you well, but you will never leave here with my treasures. If you wish to escape alive, set them down and I will let you go. You have till the count of twenty. If you haven't dropped my treasures by then, I will kill you instantly."

You and the Warrior confer in whispers. Obviously you cannot trust Mad Morwenna. But pretending to go along with her may give you time to come up with a plan.

What will you do?

If you decide to set down the treasures, turn to **PAGE 52.**

If you decide to hold on to them and see what happens next, turn to **PAGE 78.**

Suddenly, you feel hot as the outer strands of the web begin to glow. The Wizard has invoked Merlin's Fire, and the web is burning!

The spider screams and quickly climbs to its sac of eggs. The strands that bind you are beginning to burn.

"Hurry, friend," the Wizard calls as you burst free. You leap into the corner, grab the basket, then flee the burning web. As suddenly as it began, the magic of Merlin's Fire ends. Once again the room is cool and dark. You and the Wizard breathe a sigh of relief.

"Let us move quickly before the spider recovers," says the Wizard.

Shakily, you agree. You take your weapons back from the Wizard and prepare to move on.

If you now have the Crimson Crown as well as the Bottomless Basket, turn to PAGE 68.

If you have not yet won the Crimson Crown, turn to PAGE 49.

The kitchen is exactly as you remember it—except that between you and the door there are now three slavering, bloodthirsty griffins, each with the head and wings of an eagle and the body of a lion.

Their cries are deafening, but Mad Morwenna's scornful voice rises above them. "If either of you lets go of your treasure, it—and you—are lost. And you will not long be able to fight both me and my griffins!"

There is a strange popping noise in the corner of the room. There the Wizard and Mad Morwenna stand, locked in magical combat. Around them the air is flickering with colors—red, white, green, yellow—one after the other. You realize both are using every spell they know.

But you don't have time to watch their battle. Your own fight is about to begin. Like prowling lions, the griffins are closing in.

You are holding the Bottomless Basket, so you will have to fight one-handed. You must use either the sword, the lance, the flail, the dagger, or the double-headed mace.

Go to PAGE 92.

To discover the outcome of this desperate fight, flip two coins. Every time the coins come up the same (two heads or two tails), you have killed a griffin. Each time they come different (one head and one tail), you have lost a try.

You have eight tries to kill the three griffins. Now flip the coins.

If you have killed the three griffins, go on to PAGE 81.

If you have flipped the coins eight times without killing the griffins, your luck has run out. Your weapon will not protect you from Mad Morwenna's creatures. The griffins will easily defeat you now.

Close the book quickly, before they move in. And open it again the next time you are in the mood for combat, magic, and fabulous treasures.

END

At last the long quest is over. Tired but happy, you and your companion present the treasures of Ravencurse to your monarch.

"My dear friends," King Henry says, overcome with emotion, "I must admit I doubted that even you could defeat the evils of Ravencurse. You have saved me and the poor people of the realm. We cannot thank you enough."

"It is an honor to serve you," you say proudly.

Your friend nods in agreement.

"The feasting will begin at sunset," King Henry says. "I have declared a national holiday in honor of your achievement. For four days there will be celebration and merriment throughout the land."

Humbly, you and your companion thank the King for this honor.

"Afterward, on the fifth day," King Henry continues, "I must have a talk with both of you. There is a terrible problem facing us, one that only the Wizard and Warrior—" He stops, then smiles. "But more of that later. For now, it's time for pleasure and celebration!"

You and your companion look at each other knowingly. Though you will enjoy the celebration, you can scarcely wait five days . . . to discover the nature of your next perilous mission for King Henry.

END

The Wizard has gone pale. "It is an enchanted Spider of Doom," he says quietly. "This magic is so intensely focused, it may well be more powerful than mine. I fear neither spells nor weapons will work against it. Only courage and cunning will cut through this web."

"Then let me go first," you say.

Before your friend can protest, you hand him your weapons and prepare to climb through the web. As you touch it, the strands begin to vibrate with a sound like a thousand tinkling bells.

Turn to PAGE 58.

No sooner have you finished whispering the words to the spell of the Invisible Shield than you hear a whistling—the sound of a poisoned arrow flying through the air.

The Warrior is an excellent archer, you know, and a solid THUNK tells you that his arrow has hit the mark. Your spell has failed. The spider cries out in pain as the poison instantly goes to work. You feel the same pain shooting through your own body.

Ah, Wizard, it was you who prepared the poison, so you know exactly how much time you have left until the . . .

END

The Book of Spells

For use only by the WIZARD

As the Wizard, you may use any of these powerful spells. But remember, magic is mysterious and unpredictable. Use it wisely.

Spell #1: Shift Shape

This spell allows you to change shape, to assume the appearance of an animal, plant, or any object as long as it is *within view*. The spell can also be used to change the appearance of others. You cannot use this spell to change into the shape of something that is not within open view. The spell lasts for only a few minutes. It wears off suddenly, returning the subject to his or her former appearance.

Spell #2: Move Time Back

This spell allows you to move time backward. The spell can move time back one hour at the most. You can then change events by acting in a different manner during that hour. The drawback of this spell is that it's impossible to predict the precise amount of time that will be reversed— it can be anywhere from five minutes up to an hour.

Spell #3: Momentary Darkness

A sudden darkness that lasts up to five seconds is conjured up by this spell. The spell is most useful for taking someone by surprise. The darkness is total—but you must move quickly, since the darkness lasts such a short time.

Spell #4: Invisibility

A basic spell known even by apprentice sorcerers, you can use the Invisibility spell to become instantly and completely invisible.

A useful spell for fast escapes from desperate situations, it has one major drawback—the length of time the invisibility lasts cannot be predicted. It can last for as long as several weeks, or for as brief a period as a few seconds.

This spell can also be used to make an enemy or an ally invisible.

Spell #5: Invisible Shield

An invisible shield can be conjured up that completely encircles you and your companions. The shield cannot be penetrated by any weapon, although fire can be used to destroy it. The shield lasts as long as the spellcaster wishes it to. But a major drawback to this spell is that the shield is immovable. If the user moves more than a few feet in any direction, the shield disappears.

Spell #6: Mirror Image

When this spell is cast upon a foe, it causes the foe to see everything in reverse as if he or she were looking into a mirror. Especially effective for duels, this spell is used to confuse one's enemies and throw them off balance. It lasts for about five minutes.

Spell #7: Sorcerer's Sleep

This spell can be used to put anyone standing within 100 feet of you to sleep immediately. The spell can work on one person or on 500 people at once. The major drawback to this spell is that the length of time the foe will sleep cannot be predicted. It may be just for a few seconds, or a few days.

Spell #8: The Wind

This spell conjures up a hurricane force wind, strong enough to blow away the toughest foe. A most dangerous spell, it must be used with the utmost care—for once the wind has been summoned, it cannot be controlled. It may turn against the spellcaster as easily as against the persons it is intended to defeat.

Spell #9: Merlin's Fire

This spell can be used to start a blazing fire on any object. It cannot be used on people or animals. The fire burns with intensity and cannot be extinguished until the spell is removed. This is a dangerous spell because the fire can spread out of control within seconds if the wind should change directions.

(*Note*: This spell is named for Merlin but there is no known account of his having used it.)

Spell #10: Visions

This spell will cause a foe to start seeing things, all kinds of things that exist only in his or her mind! An incapacitating spell—it will cause the foe to lose all sight of what is real and what is not. Advanced wizards can even control what visions a foe will see. A difficult spell to cast, because it sometimes backfires and affects the spellcaster rather than the enemy.

Spell #11: Shrink

This spell causes a foe or foes to shrink in size. Its effect is immediate and can be used on anyone—or anything—within 100 yards. As with other spells, it is impossible to predict exactly how small someone will become or how long he or she will stay that way.

Spell #12: Combat Magic

This spell allows you to combat a magic spell that has been used against you or against a companion. It will immediately dispel any magic, except that of a Grand Wizard. This spell requires such concentration and energy that after performing it the spellcaster must rest for one entire day. *The spell can be used only once during an adventure.*

Now that you have studied your spells,
you may begin your adventure on page 14.

The Book of Weapons

For use only by the WARRIOR

As the Warrior, you may use all the weapons listed here. But remember, a great warrior uses wisdom as well as might.

Weapon #1: The Sword of the Golden Lion

An immortal sword that cannot be broken, the Sword of the Golden Lion was forged by the same swordsmith who forged the legendary Excalibur. The scabbard carries the inscription *Forever*, and a lion is etched in gold on the blade itself. You won the sword after a battle to the death against the Lancashire Sorcerer, and it has been at your side ever since.

YOU CARRY THE SWORD OF THE GOLDEN LION AT ALL TIMES. IN ADDITION, YOU MAY CHOOSE FROM THE FOLLOWING LIST THREE OTHER WEAPONS TO ACCOMPANY YOU.

Weapon #2: Battle-Axe

A favorite weapon of King Henry himself, the battle-axe can be useful when there is little room to wield a sword. With a head that weighs 20 pounds, the weight and the sharpness of its cutting edge make it a valued weapon for the knight who's strong enough to use it.

Weapon #3: Triple Crossbow

Designed especially for you by the Wizard, this crossbow has a span of three feet. It can propel three arrows at once in three different directions. This makes it especially useful in those situations when the Warrior fights alone against many.

Weapon #4: Lance

The eight-foot-long lance is an excellent weapon for battles on horseback. It is usually the weapon knights turn to when their sword has failed them. The major drawback to the lance is the fact that it can be broken.

Weapon #5: Morning Star

This weapon is guaranteed to leave its mark on a victim's memory. Sharp spikes jut out of a wooden ball, which is attached by a chain to a long wooden handle. The weapon isn't effective against armor, but is an excellent choice for inflicting head wounds.

Weapon #6: Longbow with Poison-tipped Arrows

A simple weapon, except that the poison tips were prepared especially by the Wizard. Their potency never weakens, no matter how many victims the arrows claim.

Weapon #7: Flail

Used for whipping or choking, this is largely a weapon for desperate situations. It consists of a short wooden stick attached by a long cord to a long wooden handle. Major benefit of this weapon is that it is light and easier to carry than most weapons.

Weapon #8: Double-pointed Mace

A long mace with two deadly sharp points on the head, this weapon can be slung by a loop on the wrist and used as a club, as a spear, or as a deadly lance. Many have wondered about the history of this—the only double-pointed mace in the kingdom. But you have refused to reveal its origin.

Weapon #9: Devil's Dagger

This dagger resembles a small sword except that the blade is shorter and thinner. The dagger is worn on the side opposite the sword and is usually used to deliver a death blow to someone who has already fallen. Your dagger is called the Devil's Dagger because of your superhuman skill at using it.

Now that you are suitably armed for your quest, you may begin your adventure on page 15.

About the Author

Lynn Beach has recently published a major science-fiction novel and a fantasy-adventure for young adults. Under the name Kathryn Lance, she has written several best-selling health and beauty books, including *Sportsbeauty* published by Avon Books. Ms. Beach lives in New York City.

About the Illustrator

Earl Norem has been a successful illustrator for many years. His work has appeared in Marvel Comics and Magazines, *Reader's Digest,* and many other publications. Earl and his family live in New Milford, Connecticut.